MY PET KITTEN

written by **Marilyn Baillie**

illustrated by **Jane Kurisa**

Kids Can Press

Cuddly Kittens

Hi! My name is Mittens and I'm a kitten.

Kittens come in all sorts of colors with coats in lots of patterns. Some have long hair and some have short fur. We have different shapes and sizes of ears, tails and feet. But what we all need is lots of care and lots of love.

This book is about all kittens, especially your own cute, furry friend.

There are plenty of spaces for you to fill in neat things about you and your kitten. Watch for the "Kitten Notebook" sections like this one.

Kitten Notebook

My name is _____ .

I am _____ years old.   I am a ○ girl   ○ boy

I have ____ brothers and ____ sisters.

I got this book because

○ I have always wanted a kitten

○ I just got a kitten

○ I will be getting a kitten soon

○ _____

Meow!

Believe it or not, some of my relatives are really wild. As well as the small cats people keep as pets, the cat family includes big hunters like lions, tigers, jaguars and cheetahs.

Your kitten is a member of your family and you can help keep it happy and healthy.

Be on the lookout for awesome "Meow!" sections. You'll find tips and Try This suggestions for special things you can make or do for your kitten. And look for the kitten joke!

A Great Kitten Pet

There are so many kinds of kittens you couldn't count them all! Your kitten might belong to a breed, or special group, but even kittens that are a mixture of breeds — like me! — are special in their own way. Whatever kind of kitten you have, it should be happy and healthy.

A healthy kitten
- has clear, bright eyes
- has fur that is shiny with no bare patches
- munches its food eagerly
- has been vaccinated
- is alert and friendly
- uses its litter box

Meow! Ha ha!

What do you get when you cross a kitten and a lemon?
Answer: A sourpuss!

Some people are allergic to cats, and being around me or any other kitten makes them feel sick. Keep your kitten away from anyone who is allergic to cats and we will all be happier.

Kitten Notebook

I'll try my very best to care for my kitten every day.

I'll clean its litter box

○ every day   ○ every other day

○ _____

When I need help looking after my kitten, I will ask

○ my mom   ○ my dad

○ my brother   ○ my sister

○ _____

My kitten needs its shots to stay healthy. It has

○ had its shots

○ an appointment to get its shots on this day: _____

My kitten is

○ a purebred _____   ○ a mystery mix

○ a mix that includes this breed: _____

When my kitten grows up, it will be the size of

○ a baseball   ○ a football   ○ _____

Get Ready, Get Set

Going to a new home is a giant step. It's easier for your kitten to settle in if you're prepared for it. So make sure you're ready, with these things on hand.

Play Toys

Find things for your kitten to chase or explore, like an old tennis ball or a cardboard box. Check that toys don't have loose parts your kitten might pull off and swallow.

Dinnertime

A clean food dish — two if you feed your kitten wet and dry food — and a water bowl are all you need for feeding your kitten. Find out what kind of kitten food your kitten is used to and have some at home.

Going Places

A pet carrier is a safe and easy way to carry your kitten.

Private Spaces

Kittens need a litter box with low sides so that they can climb into it. Don't forget filler for the box.

The Itch to Scratch

Kittens scratch things to keep their claws in good shape, so your kitten should have a scratching post or pad.

Meow!

Nobody has a nose like mine! My noseprint is different from every other kitten's. It's my own special mark ... just like your fingerprint is yours.

Kitten Notebook

Before my kitten's arrival, I collected these things:

- ⭕ an old towel or blanket
- ⭕ a box or basket for a bed
- ⭕ play toys
- ⭕ a litter box and filler
- ⭕ a pet carrier
- ⭕ a food dish
- ⭕ a water bowl
- ⭕ kitten food
- ⭕ a scratching post or pad
- ⭕ _____
- ⭕ _____
- ⭕ _____

I still have to get these things:

_____

_____

_____

Welcome Home, Kitten!

Your kitten's first day at home is exciting for you and a little scary for your kitten. Talk in a soft voice and watch quietly while it explores its new space. If your kitten runs and hides, wait until it peeks out at you. Soon your kitten will not feel so shy.

Happy Homecoming

Here are some first steps to welcome your kitten:

- Hold your kitten gently and whisper, "Let's be best friends!"

- Keep your kitten in a smaller room until it feels secure.

- Close drawers, closets, toilets and dryers so your kitten won't climb inside them.

- Show your kitten its litter box and where it can find its food and water.

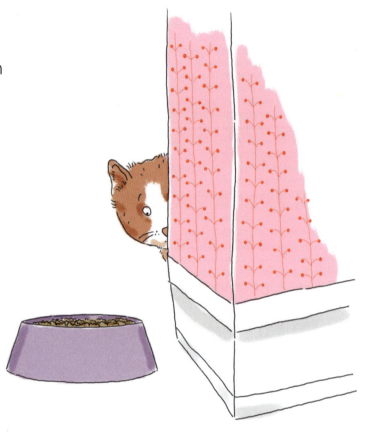

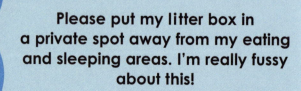

Please put my litter box in a private spot away from my eating and sleeping areas. I'm really fussy about this!

Homecoming No-nos

These are some things not to do with your new kitten:

- Don't tire your kitten out the first day.
- Don't leave small things around that your kitten can choke on.
- Don't let your kitten go into areas of your home where it is not allowed. This will only confuse it.
- Don't let your kitten outside alone.

Kitten Notebook

On my kitten's first day at home, this is what happened:

When we got home, my kitten

- ◯ stayed in the pet carrier
- ◯ found a place to hide
- ◯ ran around the kitchen
- ◯ used the litter box
- ◯ _____

My kitten's favorite place is _____ .

I can hold my kitten

- ◯ in one hand
- ◯ in two hands
- ◯ _____

My Amazing Kitten

Kitten Notebook

Here's what my new kitten looks like. I think it's the sweetest kitten in the world!

My kitten's name is _____ .

My kitten's eyes are
- ○ blue
- ○ green
- ○ yellow
- ○ _____

My kitten's nose is
- ○ black
- ○ pink
- ○ heart shaped
- ○ _____

My kitten's ears are
- ○ tall   ○ wide   ○ small   ○ folded   ○ _____

My kitten's color is
- ○ white   ○ black   ○ gray   ○ orange
- ○ a mixture of these colors: _____ _____
- ○ _____

My kitten's fur

- ○ is all one color
- ○ has stripes
- ○ has patches of these colors: _____
- ○ has these colors all mixed: _____
- ○ _____

My kitten's fur is

- ○ long and fluffy
- ○ long and thick
- ○ sleek and short
- ○ curly
- ○ _____

My kitten's whiskers are

- ○ short
- ○ long
- ○ kinky
- ○ _____

My kitten's tail is

- ○ as long as my hand
- ○ as long as my arm from my wrist to my elbow
- ○ pointy and straight
- ○ _____

My kitten has these special markings:

Kitten Care

Your kitten loves to lick and wash its fur but depends on you and your family to help keep it clean and healthy.

Litter Cleanup

Clean out your kitten's litter box often. Kittens are fussy about being clean, and your kitten might find another place to go if its litter box is full.

Grooming

Gently comb or brush your kitten from head to tail. Kittens with long hair will need to be groomed often.

Nail Care

Kittens keep their claws clean and sharp by scratching. If any nail clipping needs to be done, ask an adult or your vet to do it.

Tooth Care

If you brush your kitten's teeth, use only cat toothpaste, never your toothpaste, even if your kitten likes the smell.

Kitten Notebook

When it's time to comb my kitten's fur, my kitten

○ runs under the bed

○ stays still and purrs

○ rubs against the comb

○ _____

My kitten's tongue feels like

○ a washcloth

○ sandpaper

○ a plastic bag

○ _____

I notice my kitten licking and grooming

○ never

○ once a day

○ a few times a day

○ all the time

Meow!

Since cats wash their paws by licking them, make sure that your kitten doesn't walk in anything harmful to it. Ask an adult to help clean up any paint or cleaner spills.

Snacks and Supper

Healthy kittens need a balanced diet of kitten food each day. There is food made just for kittens, full of healthy things for your growing pet. Your kitten will be lively and have shiny fur if you and your family feed it well.

What Can My Kitten Drink?

Milk sometimes upsets kittens' stomachs. Give your kitten fresh water in its bowl each day. Then listen to it … lap, lap, lap, lap!

Meow! Try This

Kittens love to munch on green things when they can, but some houseplants can make a kitten really sick. So try growing some grass just for your pet. You can buy "cat grass" seed at a pet supply store and grow a crop that is safe and tasty for your kitten to eat.

Meow! I think people snacks are tasty, but I know they're not good for me. Your kitten will get a tummy ache if you feed it candy or junk food. And no scraps from your supper! Your kitten will be too full for its own food — and you'll be teaching your kitten bad habits.

When Should I Feed My Kitten?

Kittens need three to four small meals a day. Since their stomachs are tiny, they need to eat small amounts more often than adult cats.

Kitten Notebook

My kitten's favorite food is _____ .

My kitten won't eat _____ .

Once I found my kitten eating _____ .

My kitten takes _____ laps of water at one time.

My kitten eats

◯ at the same times every day

◯ a little at a time

◯ _____

A Perfect Kitten Day

I love to hang around at home all day and your kitten probably will, too. It will catnap on and off and take breaks to wash itself, eat and play.

Here's what makes up a happy kitten day:

1. First thing in the morning, your kitten might wake you up and ask for breakfast. When you munch on your cereal, your kitten crunches on its kitten food.

2. School time is next. Your kitten might see you off at the door, but soon it will be busy with its own day. It nibbles the food you left out and explores a little. Your kitten needs twice as much sleep as you do. It will find its own favorite spots for a catnap.

3. When you get home, your kitten might be ready to romp and play. Or maybe you'll just hang out together and relax after such a busy day.

4. Your kitten got to nap while you were at school — but you didn't! At night, when it's your bedtime, your kitten might be raring to go.

Meow!

I hate it when my food and water bowls get yucky, and so will your kitten. Wash its dishes with water and just a little soap, then rinse them well.

Kitten Notebook

In the morning, my kitten

- ○ scratches at my door
- ○ licks my face to wake me up
- ○ is still asleep
- ○ _____

When I come home from school, my kitten knows we are going to _____ .

If my kitten is asleep when I get home, it is usually

- ○ on the windowsill
- ○ on the kitchen counter
- ○ in the laundry basket
- ○ _____

My kitten's favorite part of the day is _____
_____

Sometimes my kitten and I like to do things together, like

- ○ looking at books
- ○ watching TV
- ○ napping on my bed
- ○ _____

My kitten loves it when I

- ○ scratch under its chin
- ○ rub its belly
- ○ gently pull its ears
- ○ _____

One Healthy Kitten!

Your kitten can't tell you if it's feeling sick! Here are some things you can look for when your kitten doesn't seem well. A sick kitten will
- hide and want to be left alone
- have runny or crusty eyes
- have a runny or crusty nose
- not groom itself
- not want to eat
- be more thirsty than usual
- lose weight quickly
- vomit or have diarrhea
- have a hard time breathing

If your kitten has any of these signs, ask a parent to call the vet right away.

Meow!

A regular checkup at the vet's lets my family know that I'm in the best of health and keeps me up-to-date with my vaccinations. Shots stop your kitten from catching nasty illnesses. And the vet visit gives your family a chance to ask all their kitten questions.

Kitten Notebook

Here's a healthy kitten checklist.

My kitten

- ◯ wants to play
- ◯ has shiny eyes
- ◯ is bright and alert
- ◯ has glossy fur and grooms with pride
- ◯ enjoys its food

When my kitten goes to see the veterinarian it

- ◯ hides in the pet carrier and won't come out
- ◯ cries
- ◯ sits calmly and looks at the other animals
- ◯ _____

My kitten

- ◯ has had fleas
- ◯ scratches but has not had fleas

My kitten

- ◯ has never been sick
- ◯ has felt a little sick
- ◯ had to go to the vet because _____

When my kitten got sick, I _____.

Purrs and Meows

Kittens don't need words to chat. Your kitten talks with its body, especially its face, eyes, ears, whiskers and tail. Its meows, purrs and hisses let you know what it wants to say. Here are some of the things your kitten might be saying to you.

I'm contented.

Does your kitten purr softly with its eyes half shut? Your kitten is saying, "I'm comfortable. I'm content!"

I'm a scaredy-cat.

If your kitten arches its back with its hair up and its tail held high, it looks one size larger. It would do this to fool an enemy, but the ears held back and the wide-open eyes give it all away. Your kitten is frightened and really a "scaredy-cat."

Look out!

Stay away if your kitten curls its lips back, tips its ears back and opens its mouth to hiss or spit. Your kitten is ready to attack!

Meow! Try This

Try to make your kitten smile. Have you ever noticed your kitten slowly blinking its eyes? That's its kitten smile! Now slowly blink back and it just might smile again!

I'm hungry!

A meow can mean "I'm hungry" as well as other things. You will get to know the different sounds your kitten makes and will know right away what it wants to tell you.

Kitten Notebook

I've heard my kitten meow

○ when it is hungry

○ when it wants me to notice it

○ _____

My kitten hisses when

○ it sees the dog next door

○ I startle it   ○ _____

My kitten

○ purrs, but you can't hear it   ○ doesn't purr at all

○ purrs all the time   ○ _____

When my kitten is scared, its whiskers point

○ out   ○ up   ○ down   ○ _____

I know when my kitten is happy, because it always _____ .

Kitten Play

Why are kittens so playful? They're born hunters so they love to jump, pounce, chase and grab. As you play with your kitten, try different games and toys. You'll soon discover what your kitten finds the most fun!

Toys to Try

- empty spool
- crumpled newspaper
- stuffed furry mouse
- plastic ball

If you pull a toy past your kitten as if it's running or flying away, your kitten will probably take up the chase.

Meow! Try This

I love to play hide and seek. To play a game with your kitten, all you need is an empty paper grocery bag. Lay it on the floor and your kitten might sneak right in the opening.

Toys That Hurt

Don't let your kitten play with
- small things it could swallow
- sharp things
- wool or short pieces of string
- rubber bands
- electrical cords
- tinsel Christmas decorations

Make sure to put these things out of reach.

Kitten Notebook

When I roll a ball, my kitten _____ .

My kitten can jump up

- one stair
- onto a table
- onto my bed
- _____

My kitten chases

- shadows
- light reflected from my watch
- its tail
- _____

My kitten's favorite play toy is _____ but it is not allowed to play with _____ .

23

Kitten Training

Kittens don't usually learn pet tricks. Some people say we're not smart enough, others say we're too smart to try silly tricks! But now is the time to help your kitten learn good habits before bad ones start. A soft voice and lots of love will help your kitten with its lessons.

Sharp Claws Hurt Furniture

Kittens need to scratch and sharpen their claws. They will use the furniture if you don't give them another scratching place, so make or buy a scratching post or pad.

Sharp Claws Hurt People

Sometimes your kitten might get too excited and out come the claws to grab you. If this happens, stop playing. Don't pull your hand away, because your kitten will think you are still playing. Gently push your hand towards your kitten and it will usually let go. And never yell at or hit your kitten! Yelling and hitting only teach your kitten to be afraid of you.

All cats can do an amazing thing with their claws! When we don't need them for scratching, we can pull our claws in and tuck them into our paws.

Kitten Notebook

My kitten's claws are as sharp as

- ○ a fork
- ○ a pencil
- ○ a needle
- ○ _____

Instead of using its scratching post, I caught my kitten scratching

- ○ my bedroom rug
- ○ the leg of my dad's chair
- ○ my mom's favorite cushion
- ○ _____

When my kitten sneaks up on me to pounce, I usually

- ○ hear it behind me
- ○ don't hear a thing

My kitten loves to climb

- ○ the curtains
- ○ the dining-room chairs
- ○ me
- ○ _____

Travels with Kitten

Most kittens like to stay at home, but travels with your kitten can go smoothly if you plan ahead. Make sure your kitten is used to its pet carrier, even if you are driving only a few blocks to the vet's. If you are flying, an adult will make the arrangements for your kitten with the airline.

Road Trip Tips

- Keep a small litter box in the car for your kitten.
- Bring a halter and leash so you can hang on to your kitten when you get out of the car. Don't forget to let your kitten get used to wearing the harness and being on the leash before the trip.
- Have some favorite toys on hand.
- Put a soft blanket or towel in the cat carrier.
- Do not give your kitten food or water before the trip in case of carsickness.

Meow! Try This

It's never too soon to get your kitten used to its pet carrier. Leave the carrier open so your kitten can go inside and explore. Once your kitten is happy inside the case, gently close the door. Make a game of carrying it around the house. If the kitten has fun in the carrier, it will probably run right in the carrier when it's time to take it somewhere.

Kitten Notebook

You'll need this stuff to travel with your kitten. Circle the items as you pack them:

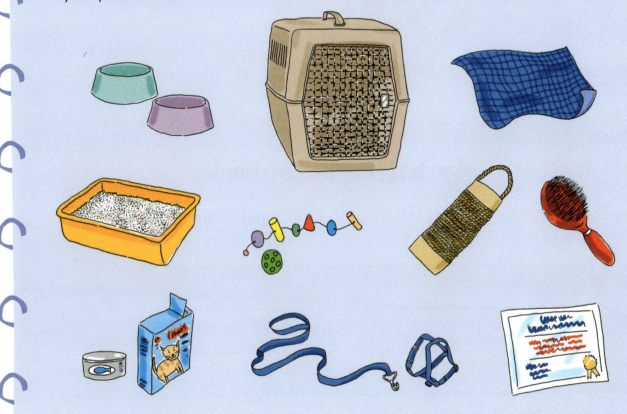

The farthest my kitten has been from our home is

○ next door   ○ across the ocean

○ another city   ○ _____

My kitten

○ hates riding in the car   ○ likes to look out the car window

○ _____

Kitten and Me

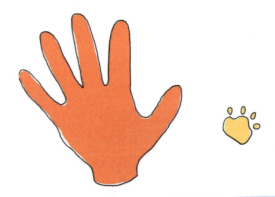

My Kitten Scrapbook

Here is a space for my best story about the cutest kitten in the world.

_____
_____
_____
_____
_____
_____
_____

My Kitten Gallery

(Draw or glue in pictures of your kitten. Write down the date and what your kitten was doing.)

Date: _____

_____
_____
_____
_____
_____

Date: _____

_____
_____
_____
_____
_____

Same Time Next Year

It's been one year since I got my kitten, and we both have changed a lot!

Kitten Notebook

My kitten has grown up into a cat, and looks like this:

I look different, too!

I am now _____ years old and am in grade ____ .

Kitten Notebook

My cat knows how to

- ○ use its litter box
- ○ scratch only the scratching post
- ○ _____
- ○ _____
- ○ _____

What I love best about my cat is _____

_____.

My cat has grown so that its head is up to the top of my

- ○ shoes
- ○ ankles
- ○ knees
- ○ _____

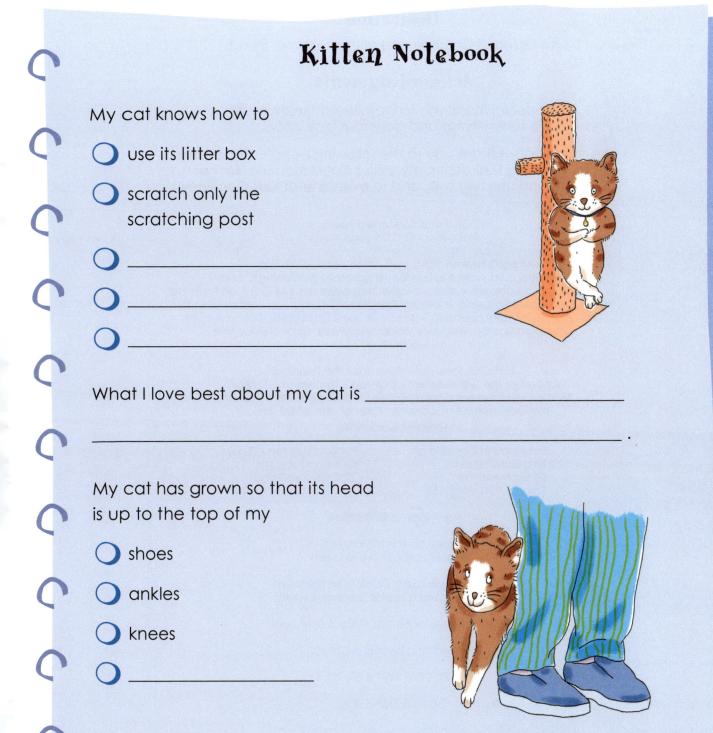

31

Dedication

For Cali and Christine and all their animal friends

Acknowledgments

A special thank you to Dr. Richard Medhurst for
his expertise and generous assistance.

An appreciative thank you to the following people: Jane Kurisu
for her lively illustrations; my editor, Kat Mototsune, for her
creative and unerring eye; and to everyone at Kids Can Press.

Text © 2005 Marilyn Baillie
Illustrations © 2005 Jane Kurisu

All rights reserved. No part of this publication may
be reproduced, stored in a retrieval system or transmitted, in any
form or by any means, without the prior written permission of Kids Can Press Ltd.
or, in case of photocopying or other reprographic copying, a license from The
Canadian Copyright Licensing Agency (Access Copyright). For an Access
Copyright license, visit www.accesscopyright.ca or call toll free
to 1-800-893-5777.

Kids Can Press acknowledges the financial
support of the Government of Ontario, through the Ontario
Media Development Corporation's Ontario Book Initiative, and
the Government of Canada, through the BPIDP, for our
publishing activity.

Published in Canada by	Published in the U.S. by
Kids Can Press Ltd.	Kids Can Press Ltd.
29 Birch Avenue	2250 Military Road
Toronto, ON M4V 1E2	Tonawanda, NY 14150

www.kidscanpress.com

Edited by Kat Mototsune
Designed by Kathleen Collett

Veterinary Consultant: Dr. Richard Medhurst,
Rosedale Animal Hospital, Toronto, Ontario

Cover and interior photos © Stockbyte.com

Printed and bound in China

CM PA 05 0 9 8 7 6 5 4 3 2 1

ISBN 1-55337-653-6

Kids Can Press is a Corus™ Entertainment company